Mr Babbit's Rabbit

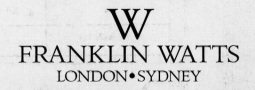

Written by
Penny Dolan

Illustrated by
Tomislav Zlatic

W
FRANKLIN WATTS
LONDON·SYDNEY

Penny Dolan
"I met a class where almost everyone owned a pet rabbit! They told me rabbits are extremely good at escaping."

Tomislav Zlatic
"I used to have a hedgehog called Jez. He lived on my balcony. I thought he liked it, but one day he ran away ... maybe to a bigger balcony!"

Mr Babbit had a rabbit.

He kept her in a hutch.

But Mr Babbit's rabbit
didn't like it very much.

7

Out jumped the rabbit ...

8

... and away she ran.

10

So off ran Mr Babbit
with his watering can.

13

They ran through the gate.

They ran down the lane.

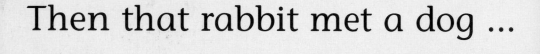

Then that rabbit met a dog ...

17

... and she raced
back home again!

Now Mr Babbit's rabbit
has a much bigger hutch.

21

And both she and Mr Babbit
like it ever so much!